KIDS CAN'T ~~~
THE CH~~~~ ~~~~
OWN ADVENTURE® STORIES!

"Choose Your Own Adventure is the best thing that has come along since books themselves."
—Alysha Beyer, age 11

"I didn't read much before, but now I read my Choose Your Own Adventure books almost every night."
—Chris Brogan, age 13

"I love the control I have over what happens next."
—Kosta Efstathiou, age 17

"Choose Your Own Adventure books are so much fun to read and collect—I want them all!"
—Brendan Davin, age 11

And teachers like this series, too:
"We have read and reread, worn thin, loved, loaned, bought for others, and donated to school libraries our Choose Your Own Adventure books."

CHOOSE YOUR OWN ADVENTURE®—
AND MAKE READING MORE FUN!

Bantam Books in the Choose Your Own Adventure® series
Ask your bookseller for the books you have missed

EARTHQUAKE!

BY ALISON GILLIGAN

ILLUSTRATED BY HAL FRENCK

An R.A. Montgomery Book

BANTAM BOOKS
NEW YORK • TORONTO • LONDON • SYDNEY • AUCKLAND

RL 4, age 10 and up

EARTHQUAKE!
A Bantam Book / November 1992

*CHOOSE YOUR OWN ADVENTURE® is a registered trademark
of Bantam Books, a division of Bantam Doubleday Dell Publishing
Group, Inc. Registered in U.S. Patent and Trademark Office
and elsewhere.*

Original conception of Edward Packard

*Cover art by James Warhola
Interior illustrations by Hal Frenck*

ISBN 0-553-29299-4

Published simultaneously in the United States and Canada

*Bantam Books are published by Bantam Books, a division of Bantam
Doubleday Dell Publishing Group, Inc. Its trademark, consisting of
the words "Bantam Books" and the portrayal of a rooster, is Regis-
tered in U.S. Patent and Trademark Office and in other countries.
Marca Registrada. Bantam Books, 666 Fifth Avenue, New York, New
York 10103.*

PRINTED IN THE UNITED STATES OF AMERICA

OPM   0 9 8 7 6 5 4 3 2 1

For Mag and for Shannon

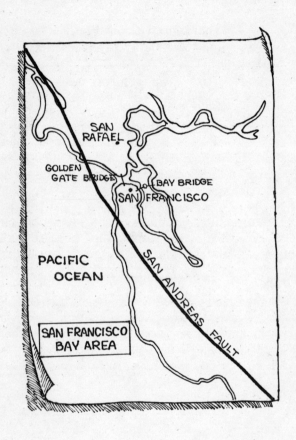

SAN
RAFAEL

GOLDEN
GATE BRIDGE

BAY BRIDGE

SAN FRANCISCO

PACIFIC
OCEAN

SAN ANDREAS FAULT

SAN FRANCISCO
BAY AREA

WARNING!!!

Do not read this book straight through from beginning to end. These pages contain many different adventures that you may have when an earthquake hits while you're visiting San Francisco. From time to time as you read along, you will be asked to make a choice. Your choice may lead to success or disaster!

The adventures you have are the results of your choices. You are responsible because you choose! After you make a choice, follow the instructions to find out what happens to you next.

Think carefully before you make a decision. In the aftermath of the quake, San Francisco lies in ruins, and danger waits around every corner. Many lives hang in the balance. You may become a hero—or you may never make it home alive.

Good luck!

You're seated on a new Boeing 767 bound for San Francisco. You're on your way to visit your best friend, Maxwell McCurt. Growing up together in Vermont, you and Max were inseparable. But a year ago his father got a job offer in San Francisco, and the McCurts decided to move. Max now has a summer internship as a research assistant at the San Francisco Zoological Gardens, otherwise known as the zoo.

From what he's told you, Max works with all sorts of advanced computer programs to study animal behavior. You're excited to go and help him out. You're also looking forward to seeing your best friend. This visit will be the first time you've seen him since his family moved.

An hour into the flight you happen to glance at a paper the woman sitting next to you is reading. It's titled "On the Breaking Edge of Earthquakes: New Theories in Seismology." You've always been a little curious about earthquakes, and since you're heading into the heart of earthquake country, you decide to ask her what "seismology" is.

"Most people understand very little about seismology—or seismologists," your seatmate says. The twinkle in her deep blue eyes reveals the excitement she has for her work. "Seismology is the scientific study of earthquakes; seismologists are those of us who study quakes and how to predict them." She shakes your hand. "Allow me to introduce myself. I'm Professor Lynn Bailey, head of the Stiles Seismology Lab."

Turn to page 2.

You're not sure, but you think you've heard Professor Bailey's name on TV, in connection with news reports of recent tremors in and around San Francisco. The tremors worried your parents so much they almost didn't let you take this trip. "So the reason San Francisco is prone to earthquakes is because of its location near the San Andreas Fault?" you ask her.

"You're well-informed," Professor Bailey says, obviously impressed. "Earthquakes occur along geologic fault lines and are caused by subterranean volcanic forces. San Francisco happens to be right on the edge of a continental plate. That's why we seismologists flock there. We're all hoping to predict the 'Big One'; the next earthquake of the magnitude of the famous San Francisco earthquake of 1906."

"Your work sounds pretty exciting," you say. "How do you tell if a quake is coming?"

"There are two new theories about prediction," Professor Bailey replies. "The one I subscribe to measures the emission of radon gas from the earth. A sudden increase in radon gas signals that an earthquake is imminent."

"And the other?" you ask.

"An old wives' tale," she scoffs. "Some New Age nut case, Dr. Fairnsworth Orion, got a two-million-dollar grant to study the behavior of zoo animals in order to determine if they get all jittery before a tremor. It's quite ridiculous, really. What's worse is that Orion is my main rival for the Whitbread Prize."

Go on to the next page.

"The Whitbread Prize?" you ask.

"It's given to the person in the field making the greatest advances in seismology," she says eagerly. "The one who wins it will have the freedom to study and work and travel without ever having to worry about money again."

For the rest of the trip Professor Bailey keeps you spellbound with her tales of destruction surrounding recent earthquakes and her methods of predicting them.

As the plane is coming in for a landing, she says, "The Stiles lab is in the WhitVic Research Center in San Francisco. If you're interested, I'll be glad to give you and your friend a tour of our facilities."

"I'd love to visit," you say. Since Monday is your friend Max's day off, you arrange for the two of you to meet Professor Bailey at the lab on Monday morning.

"We're in the basement," she explains. "Closer to the earth's core—that's our motto." She laughs. "Actually, we've got emissions testing equipment down there, with a data collection center on the second floor. We're monitoring radon emissions from five spots in greater San Francisco, twelve spots along the San Andreas Fault, and three along the coast."

Turn to page 30.

4

A week later, after you've checked on your friends and the chaos has died down, you visit Farley McEachron in his hospital suite. The paramedic wasn't kidding: Mr. McEachron is extremely wealthy and he makes good on his promise to you.

"I told you I'd be forever grateful for your help," he says brightly, "and I am." He hands you and Max thin envelopes bearing his family crest. You rip yours open in surprise and anticipation. You can't believe your eyes.

"A hundred thousand dollars," Max says in shock.

"It's for your education," Farley interrupts, grinning from ear to ear. "An education helped me get to where I am today. I want you two to have the same opportunity."

You and Max turn toward each other and smile gleefully. A photographer quickly snaps your picture. Tomorrow morning your story will be on the front page of every newspaper from coast to coast!

The End

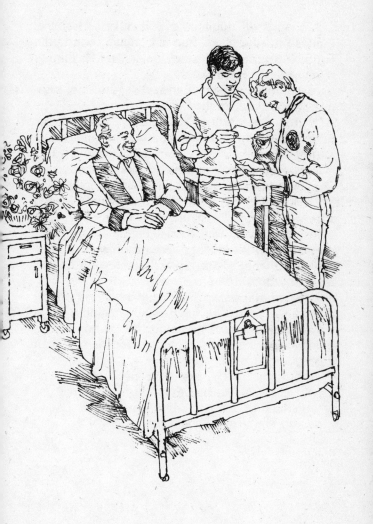

"Hey, you!" you hear as you enter the terminal building. Your friend Max is running toward you, grinning from ear to ear, looking much thinner than he did a year ago.

"You haven't gained an ounce," he says, slapping you hard on the back.

"And you," you reply, smiling. "You've lost a ton!" Back in Vermont Max was always one of the chubbiest kids in school. Now, although he's still stocky, he is trimmer and more muscular.

"Almost thirty pounds," he says happily. "I've taken up jogging, swimming, and tennis. Needed to have a physique to match the brains. Very Californian, you know." You laugh. Max looks great. And he wasn't kidding about the brains, either. He's terrific in science; practically a genius.

"My mom's here somewhere," Max declares, searching the crowd. "We're going to hop in the car and zoom into town. Dad's meeting us at Zuni Café and Grill for dinner. You're gonna love this place. Full-course Italian. You've got your pasta, your meat, your fish . . . "

You grin and shake your head. One thing you've always loved about Max—he may be something of a science nerd, but he sure knows how to appreciate great food.

Turn to page 27.

You, Max, and Ollie race to the Rain Forest Hall. Inside the exhibit it's cool now instead of hot and steamy. Looking up, you notice that many of the glass roof panels have shattered. You hope the puff adder's cage didn't break, too. You keep an eye out, not wanting to step on the deadly snake.

As you pass the adder's cage you see that it *has* shattered, and you watch in horror as a long scaly tail slides through a narrow break in the lemur cage. Through the cracked glass you can see that both lemurs are backed up against the wall, standing completely still, the hair raised straight up on the backs of their necks. The adder slithers toward them slowly. Max comes up beside you and gasps.

"We've got to do something," you whisper urgently. "We can't let the adder get them, or the species really could become extinct."

Just then, in the distance, you hear Sitruc roar. You hope he's not roaring at Dr. Orion.

If you choose to stop and try to save the lemurs, turn to page 31.

If you decide to continue your search for Dr. Orion immediately, turn to page 42.

Cautiously you and Max maneuver the stretcher out the narrow doorway and down the hall. Ollie is in the lead. He is nimble on his paws, picking his way through the earthquake's debris.

Once you reach the stairway you glance down at the professor. She is a frightening shade of white. "Step on it," you bark at Max. Without looking back, he picks up his pace.

Just as you reach the stairwell, a slow rumble begins, building in intensity. Max pauses under the doorframe, wincing at the aftershock. It soon passes, and he begins leading you up the cracked stairs.

With greater speed you push through the side entrance of the building and into the alley. Max pauses and looks back at the professor. She is barely breathing.

Turn to page 70.

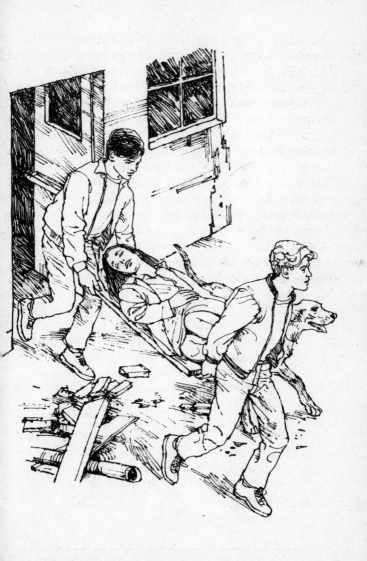

On Sunday afternoon, your sightseeing takes you to the San Francisco Marina. Standing outside a fried-clam stand near the marina, you feel a sudden violent shaking beneath your feet. For a second your knees buckle—you can barely stand. The shaking continues for five seconds, then suddenly stops. When you look around, everyone seems calm. Have you imagined it? You look at Ollie, who seems to be shaking slightly. Max pauses between bites of clam strips. "An earth tremor," he says nonchalantly. "They happen a lot. Poor Ollie goes nuts every time."

"A tremor!" you exclaim. "You mean an earthquake?"

"A very minor one," Max replies. "You get used to them living out here. It doesn't mean the Big One's around the corner, you know."

"I wonder if Professor Bailey's radon readings just shot up," you say.

"Her what?" Max asks sharply. You tell him about meeting Professor Bailey and give him a brief outline of her work.

"I've heard about her from a guy I work with at the zoo in the research department," says Max. "He may seem a little weird at first, but he's really brilliant. He's working on a theory to predict earthquakes by variations in animal behavior: some animals seem to become restless *before* tremors hit. It's revolutionary work. He's up for a major grant and . . . "

Go on to the next page.

"His name's not Orion, is it?" you ask. "Are you talking about the Whitbread Prize?"

"So you've heard of him! And the prize," Max says, amazed. "His work isn't very well known yet, but he's close to making a major break-through."

"Professor Bailey seems to be on the verge of something big, too," you say, "and she said she'd tell us about it tomorrow when we visit her lab."

"Cool," says Max. "Dr. Orion talks about Professor Bailey as if she's the enemy. I'd like to see what she's really like."

Turn to page 34.

Time is of the essence. "We'll just have to risk running the bridge," you tell Max. You gauge the strength of the wind and perform some quick mental calculations.

"The way I see it," you say cautiously, "the head wind is about fifteen knots. With a maximum engine speed of sixty knots per hour from a starting distance of forty-five feet, it should only take four point three seconds to pass under the bridge, allowing for wave clearance as well."

"All right," Max agrees. "I'll back her up sixty feet for a running start." He turns the boat westward and slowly circles to get in position. Glancing over your shoulder you see the barge captain smile and wave good-bye. He must think you're turning back. If he only knew.

Go on to the next page.

When Max is about sixty feet from the bridge, he puts the boat into idle, waits about five seconds for a gust of wind to pass, then throws the accelerator forward for maximum speed. With a jolt the little boat screams ahead. Ollie's ears blow backward in the wind like banners.

The barge captain turns and stares in disbelief. He's too startled even to speak. It's just as well. As you zoom forward, the last thing you want to hear are more words of warning.

About ten feet in front of the barge you watch in terror as the bridge sways five feet forward and eight feet back. It looks as if it's about to snap! Max keeps his hand on the accelerator and stubbornly stares ahead.

Turn to page 104.

Max watches Ollie for a second and then jumps out of bed to comfort the dog. "Ollie never paces like this," he says. "We've got to take him to Dr. Orion for observation first thing tomorrow morning! The zoo's closed on Monday for renovation, but Dr. Orion will probably be there anyway. I think he'll be interested in Ollie's behavior. The way he's been pacing reminds me of the way the Bengal tigers at the zoo have been acting lately."

"Meaning what?" you ask, but you're afraid you already know the answer.

"Meaning the Big One could be just around the corner," Max replies. "We don't have any time to waste. We'll just have to go and see your friend Professor Bailey another time."

"But if a quake is coming, Professor Bailey might be able to tell us exactly when and where," you say. "Her radon readings are very precise. Maybe we should go to the lab first, and then take Ollie to the zoo if she says it's safe."

"Let's sleep on it and see how Ollie is in the morning," says Max. "Let me know what you want to do then."

If you decide to take Ollie to the zoo for Dr. Orion to observe, turn to page 25.

If you decide to keep your appointment with Professor Bailey, turn to page 58.

You spend the rest of the morning helping Max finish a computer program meant to track the nocturnal habits of the zoo animals. There are video monitors strategically placed in certain cages to monitor animal movements. Dr. Orion is particularly excited about Sitruc's behavior.

"I plan to spend the afternoon inside the tiger cage," he says when you are leaving to keep your appointment with Professor Bailey. "I want to be able to communicate with the animals as one—to feel what they feel, to develop my animal sense."

Turn to page 67.

The lemurs quietly crawl over to you. One of them burrows its nose into your chest, as if it is trying to prod you awake. But it's no use. The adder's poison is traveling through your system. You begin to feel numb all over. Your only thought is that at least now the lemurs will be spared. As if from a great distance you hear Max calling out your name. It's the last sound you'll ever hear.

The End

Max tells Dr. Orion about Ollie's odd behavior. "Very interesting," he says, stroking his beard. "And I'm impressed that you could read the dog's emotions," he says to you. "I feel a good aura surrounding your being. You have a gift for communicating with animals." You stifle a laugh. You can't believe that this guy is for real.

Dr. Orion takes a break from his studies and gives you a personal tour of the zoo. You visit the Bear Grotto where kodiak, spectacled, and polar bears, ranging in size from eight hundred to twelve hundred pounds, frolic lazily near a stone waterfall. Then it's on to visit some reptiles. You hate snakes, and you wrinkle your nose in disgust as you follow Dr. Orion and Max into the dark interior of a nearby building.

"Brewster," Dr. Orion calls out to a small, dark-haired man with a garter snake coiled around his wrist. "How about a quick snake-holding demonstration for my young friends." Max eagerly approaches Brewster. But you're not quite as anxious to touch the reptile.

"You handle snakes very gently but firmly," says Brewster. "First you grasp their heads to prevent them from biting. Then you grab their tails to immobilize them." Brewster expertly demonstrates his technique. "Now for lunch," he says. You watch in disgust as he feeds a small rat to the snake. It is swallowed whole.

Go on to the next page.

Dr. Orion smiles as he watches your face. "All species of snakes—and there are over twenty-seven hundred species worldwide—eat their food without chewing. Fascinating creatures. They're also totally deaf, sensing ground vibrations as a means of detecting enemies or prey. Snakes are extremely important to my research right now. Especially the zoo's Rainbow Boa, Fang. He's extremely temperamental, but he's a very sensitive creature."

Turn to page 41.

Cautiously you enter the room where Zooey, the other Bengal tiger, is held. There are no glass barriers here, only a large iron cage to house the pregnant tigress. "Dr. Orion?" you call. You spot Zooey lying motionless, on her back, in the far corner of her cage. You can hear her breath coming in short, quick gasps.

There is a sudden movement to your left. You can feel hot breath on the back of your neck. Very slowly you turn and look into the yellow eyes of Sitruc. He stares back at you, his face intense and watchful. The tiger is only about a foot away. Your ears are ringing and your heart is beating very fast. For a moment you forget to breathe.

Max holds his tranquilizer gun at the ready, reluctant to use it unless he has to.

"Proceed with caution," a voice says from the dark recesses of the room. You peer toward the noise. "It's me," Dr. Orion says quietly. "I knew you'd come to help."

Turn to page 28.

22

Dr. Orion winds up the tour at the Lion House, a sprawling granite structure surrounded by fields meant to simulate the plains of Africa.

"Come see this," Dr. Orion says excitedly. You follow him into the dark recesses of the structure. You hear the quiet, rhythmic pacing of a large, restless animal. Peering through the darkness, you see an enormous male tiger striding back and forth. The tiger gracefully comes to a stop and eyes you intensely.

"This is the zoo's pride and joy," Dr. Orion whispers in hushed tones. "Sitruc, a rare Bengal tiger from India, Latin name *Panthera tigris*. He's about nine and a half feet tall when he stands on his hind legs. He may look fierce, but he's really just a pussycat."

"Sitruc's mate, Zooey, is about to deliver a litter of cubs," Dr. Orion continues quietly. "The zookeeper thinks that's why he's pacing so much. But I'm convinced it relates to my theory about animal behavior immediately preceding an earthquake. Fingers crossed that I'm right." You nod politely, but you're not sure you share his hope.

Turn to page 15.

"We'll compromise," you tell Professor Bailey. Max nods in agreement. "We'll carry you out of here, but the second we get you safely outside, we'll sneak back in and go to the data collection center."

You know Professor Bailey is too weak to argue anymore. Ollie nudges her with his nose. She sighs deeply and shuts her eyes.

"We'd better hurry," Max tells you. "She doesn't look good." You begin ripping up a canvas lab coat while Max pries apart a wooden bookcase. In a few minutes time you secure Professor Bailey to a makeshift stretcher and quickly lift her to shoulder height. The adrenaline in your system makes Professor Bailey feel as light as a feather.

Turn to page 8.

Suddenly the rumbling slows, then stops. For a second you hear nothing but silence, then pure chaos. People are screaming everywhere—out on the street, from their cars, and from the windows of nearby buildings. The sign that almost crushed you has fallen on an old man instead, pinning him beneath it.

"We have to help that man!" you shout to Max. "That could have been us under that sign!"

"But what about Dr. Orion?" asks Max. "He's in the tiger cage with Sitruc. Sitruc's a huge, dangerous predator. Even though Orion works with him every day, who knows what might happen if Sitruc's injured and upset! We've got to go back to the zoo right away. I think I hear sirens—I'm sure emergency rescue workers will get here soon."

Every second counts. You've got to decide what you're going to do, fast.

If you choose to help the old man pinned down by the sign, turn to page 43.

If you choose to run immediately to the zoo to help Dr. Orion, turn to page 32.

Ollie isn't quite as nervous in the morning, but you decide that the way he behaved last night was too strange to ignore. You call Professor Bailey to reschedule your appointment for the afternoon and head for the zoo with Ollie in tow.

As you pass under the zoo's wrought iron gates you leave the busy city behind and enter a world of exotic plants and animals. You are struck by the beauty of your surroundings—the lush vegetation and the discreet barriers holding the animals in their natural pens. It's almost as if there were no cages and the animals roamed free, just like in the real jungle. The zoo is closed to the public today in preparation for the grand opening of a new rain forest exhibit. Walking around, you feel like you and Max are the only humans around. Max's voice jars you back to reality.

"Pretty impressive, huh?" he says with pride. "This way—I want to introduce you to my mentor, Dr. Fairnsworth Orion."

Turn to page 36.

Over the weekend Max plays tour guide, showing you the highlights of San Francisco. You visit the fresh seafood stands at Fisherman's Wharf and take the elevator to the top of Coit Tower, where you look out on Alcatraz, the old prison island where the famous "Bird Man" spent over fifty years behind bars. In the elevator you and Max put on tough faces, pretending to be Clint Eastwood in *Escape from Alcatraz*.

Later you take a ride on one of the city's famous cable cars, then stroll through Chinatown, where you sample dim sum dumplings. The waiters wheel around carts and yell out the names of the dumplings as they go by.

On Sunday morning you have a great time sailing in the bay on Max's father's new boat.

As you're sightseeing, Max's trusty dog Ollie is always by your side. Ollie is part Labrador retriever, part dalmatian, and quite a character. Part of you suspects Ollie's attentiveness has to do with the fact that Max is always getting him an extra side order of food. But you can also tell that Ollie is a good, loyal friend.

Turn to page 10.

You and Max slowly back away from the tiger and toward Dr. Orion's voice. He is lying on the hard concrete floor, immobilized by a shard of metal pipe that has pinned his arm to the wall behind him. You gasp at the sight of the metal protruding from his skin just above the elbow.

"One of the water pipes burst in the quake and got me. But it's not nearly as bad as it looks," he says, trying to sound reassuring. "I can still move my fingers. I don't think there'll be any permanent damage. But I'm pinned here until medical help arrives."

Max falls to his knees and pulls off his sweatshirt. He uses it to apply direct pressure to Dr. Orion's arm, trying to stop the bleeding.

"Is there anything I can do?" you ask.

"Help Zooey," Orion says, his voice pleading. "She appears to have gone into premature labor, probably as a result of the quake. Go to her and measure her heartbeats per minute. I'll talk you through the rest."

"Shouldn't I get some help for you first?" you ask nervously. "That arm doesn't look too great."

Go on to the next page.

"Don't worry about me now," Dr. Orion insists. "I'll be all right. Now hurry. The key to Zooey's cage is on a hook outside the door."

You want to listen to Dr. Orion and help Zooey with her delivery. But part of you feels you should get help for Dr. Orion first.

If you go to look for help for Dr. Orion, turn to page 52.

If you follow his instructions, turn to page 46.

"How's the testing going?" you ask, wondering if her radon readings show any signs of coming tremors.

"It's coming along well," she replies seriously. "Maybe too well . . ."

Just then the wheels of the plane touch down, reminding you that you are going to be right on top of the San Andreas Fault for the next month. You hope the readings don't mean an earthquake will hit before you leave! Professor Bailey shakes your hand and offers you her business card. "I'll tell you all about my tests when you visit," she says, getting out of her seat and heading down the aisle.

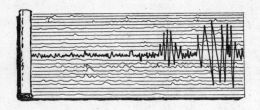

Turn to page 6.

You decide you can't let the lemurs fall prey to the deadly adder.

"It'll only take a minute to save the lemurs," you tell Max. "Then we can run straight over to the Lion House. After all, we don't even know for sure that Dr. Orion is in trouble."

"Okay," Max says. "Let's hurry up with this rescue mission."

Only part of the glass barrier enclosing the lemur house has shattered, leaving a small opening. The edges of the glass are razor sharp. You are able to slip through the gap easily. However, even though Max is in good shape these days, he's still quite a bit larger than you. He looks at the narrow opening doubtfully.

"I could attempt it," he says. "Maybe if I moved through with my feet first and then . . ."

"No," you interrupt. "Don't risk it. I'd rather have you safe on the outside in case you need to get help for me."

Max nods, looking slightly relieved. "All right. But be careful in there."

Turn to page 84.

The thought of Sitruc crazed by the shock of the earthquake is too frightening to ignore. "You're right," you tell Max. "Paramedics will arrive here soon to help, but we're the only ones who know that Dr. Orion is in the Lion House. Since the zoo's closed today, there won't be anyone there to help him. It's up to us to save him."

You and Max race back toward the zoo with Ollie at your heels. As soon as you spot the twisted wrought iron gates at the entrance you know that the zoo has been badly hit by the quake. Glancing around, you're alarmed to see that many of the enclosures have been damaged. You try not to think what kinds of dangerous creatures could be running around loose. Max races ahead of you into the research office, which has escaped serious damage. Just as you catch up, he emerges. "No sign of Dr. Orion in there," he says worriedly. He holds up a riflelike device. "But I picked up an emergency tranquilizer gun. It may come in handy."

You nod.

"Come on," Max continues. "We don't have a second to lose. We've got to get to the Lion House. Let's take a shortcut through the Rain Forest Hall."

Turn to page 7.

Later that night, you're lying on the extra bed in Max's room, exhausted from your weekend of sightseeing. But Max is keeping you up talking about Dr. Orion and seismology, and about your upcoming visit to Professor Bailey's lab.

As Max is talking, you begin to notice that Ollie is acting strangely. He refuses to lie at the foot of Max's bed. Instead he's walking around the perimeter of the room.

You interrupt Max's monologue. "Look at Ollie," you say. "Do you think he's okay?" Just then Ollie pauses, turns toward Max, and lets out a big yawn.

"He's just tired," Max replies, crawling under the covers. "Maybe I shouldn't have given him such a large portion of chicken lo mein for dinner."

Turn to page 64.

You just can't bring yourself to grab the adder. You've always hated snakes, and you'd do almost anything rather than touch this one.

You're quick. If you can just pull the lemurs out of the snake's reach, you'll be fine.

You move forward cautiously until the lemurs are only two feet away. The adder is completely motionless, watching your every move.

Now! You leap forward and grab both lemurs. But you're not fast enough. With surprising speed the adder lunges toward you, and you feel its sharp fangs pierce the skin on your forearm.

You drop the lemurs, and they race toward the far corner and huddle together in fear. The adder's fangs feel as if they're locked onto your arm. You flail your arm desperately, trying to end the swift, unbearable pain as the snake's deadly venom seeps into your veins. As you whirl around, the adder's body slams forcefully into the wall, and you feel its grip on your arm loosen. The snake falls into a crumpled mess on the ground. For a moment, you stand motionless. The cage begins to spin. You fall to your knees, too weak to stand.

Turn to page 17.

You find Dr. Orion roaming the zoo, checking on various animals. He grasps your hand in both of his, gazing intently into your eyes. He's a big, burly man with a substantial stomach. His long, curly brown hair melts into his heavy beard, giving him the appearance of a happy-go-lucky caveman. No wonder this guy gets along with animals, you think to yourself. He could be the missing link.

Turn to page 18.

"Maybe they already got out," Max says hopefully. Ollie sniffs at a heavy metal door and begins barking. Just then you hear a faint call for help from behind the door. Together you frantically begin pushing, trying to open it a few inches. Something has fallen behind the door and forced it shut.

"Professor Bailey!" you yell. "Is that you?" For a second there's nothing but silence. Then you hear another cry for help.

"Come on," Max says, pushing a large metal table from across the hall. You both get behind the table and, at the count of three, push with all your might. With a sudden loud crunch of metal, the door swings open two feet. Ollie runs inside, still barking. You squeeze through into the inner darkness after him.

"Hello," you call out hopefully.

"Over here," a voice calls back. You and Max stumble toward the sound. You bang your shin painfully on what feels like an overturned metal file cabinet. You grope around in the dark, and suddenly a hand grasps yours. It's Professor Bailey.

"Help me!" she says. "This fell on me and I can't move."

Go on to the next page.

With extreme care you and Max pull the cabinet into a standing position. In the dim light, you can't see the extent of Professor Bailey's injuries, but she's in bad shape. She seems to be on the verge of losing consciousness.

"We've got to carry Professor Bailey out of here," Max tells you quietly. "This building won't last much longer if there's an aftershock."

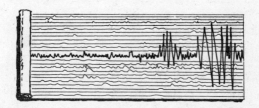

Turn to page 66.

Next on the tour is the zoo's brand-new rain forest exhibit, scheduled to open to the public tomorrow. A large climate-controlled glass dome traps the humidity characteristic of rain forests, giving the exhibit a steamy, tropical feeling. Max leads you to his favorite animals in the exhibit, a pair of extremely rare lemurs. They look like small, exotic monkeys.

"These are on the endangered species list," Dr. Orion says quietly. You watch as the graceful animals swing back and forth between branches. "We're hoping they'll breed and produce a litter soon. Eventually the zoo hopes to be able to release the lemurs back into the wild, where they can repopulate the rain forest. The lemur population is down to almost nothing due to development."

You notice a large snake in a glass cage immediately to the left of the lemurs. Dr. Orion catches your eye. "A puff adder," he says. "One of the deadliest snakes in the world."

"Why is it right next to the lemurs?" you ask.

"Well, they're natural neighbors," Dr. Orion says. "They live in the same fragile ecosystem."

"They don't look like very friendly neighbors," you comment under your breath. You're glad the glass walls of the cage are so thick.

Turn to page 22.

You turn to Max "We'll just get ourselves killed if we get in the way of a puff adder. Anyway, Dr. Orion's life is more important than those lemurs, no matter how rare they are. Let's go!" You sprint the rest of the way to the Lion House, the image of the adder silently waiting for the lemurs to make a wrong move haunting you.

Once inside the house you look around nervously. Most of the cages seem to have survived the quake, although a few have dangerously large cracks running through the glass barriers. You walk through the room as panthers and leopards watch you curiously.

As soon as you enter the main room you know that something is wrong. The glass from these cages has shattered and lies in shards on the floor. Glancing to your left you realize that Sitruc's cage is empty. He's escaped! And there's no sign of Dr. Orion. "What now?" you ask Max.

As if in answer, Sitruc lets out an enormous roar. By the sound of it, the huge tiger is dangerously close—perhaps in the next room.

"Of course!" Max says quickly. "Sitruc's mate, Zooey, is kept in the next room. Sitruc and Dr. Orion must be in there." Together you race forward. Ollie follows close behind.

Turn to page 20.

You can't just leave this old man. He's suffering right in front of you.

"Hurry, Max," you say, running toward the old man. "We'll go check if Dr. Orion is okay as soon as we help out here." You and Max struggle to lift the fallen sign from the man's legs. Ollie joins in the rescue effort, nudging the heavy sign with his nose. Together the three of you are finally able to shove the sign aside. The man gasps in pain.

"I'll be forever grateful to you," the old man says in a whisper. Gently, you grasp his hand. He looks a little like your grandfather.

"It's what anyone would do," you say modestly. You can hear the sound of sirens getting closer. "Just lie still. An ambulance will be here soon."

"I am grateful. I'd like to make it up to you," he says hoarsely. "As soon as I recover, I promise to . . ."

The man's whisper is cut short by Max's yelling. "Over here," he calls. A paramedic is climbing out of the ambulance that has just pulled up to the curb. "He's badly hurt—his legs look like they've been crushed."

The paramedic drops to his feet and begins to examine the old man. With sudden surprise he cries, "Farley McEachron! You boys have rescued Farley McEachron—one of the city's wealthiest and kindest philanthropists." The old man smiles, embarrassed.

Turn to page 4.

"This is it!" Max yells. "Look." The lines from the second graph are much bigger, with several high peaks following the initial quake.

"And they're getting bigger," you shout in alarm. "Look at the paper coming out now. These lines are all over the place." Ollie barks, sensing your excitement.

Max reads the emissograph's location tag. "San Rafael, California. That's about twenty-five miles from here, across the Golden Gate Bridge."

"From the looks of that graph, we haven't much time," you yell to him, running toward the stairwell.

Once you hit the street you find a search and rescue team and direct them to Professor Bailey. Then you're off on foot, with Ollie beside you, racing after Max as he heads toward the waterfront.

Turn to page 78.

You decide to do as Dr. Orion said and help Zooey. A thought occurs to you. Perhaps you can send Ollie to bring back assistance. Dr. Orion said you had a way with animals. You guess it's worth a try.

You walk over to the dog and hold his head in your hands.

"Ollie" you say, feeling a bit foolish. "Listen closely. Go out and find help. Fast. And bring them back here quickly. Dr. Orion's in trouble. We need help. Now."

As if he understands completely, Ollie pulls back and quickly runs from the room. You look over toward Max. The look of fear on his face tells you Dr. Orion is in more trouble than he pretends to be. The blood loss must be quite severe. While Max mops sweat from Dr. Orion's brow, you take a deep breath and enter Zooey's cage, locking it behind you. Sitruc stands guard outside the cage. He seems to understand that you are there to help.

Turn to page 61.

Max steers the boat to the wharf's pier, and you and Ollie scramble ashore with Max behind you. With every passing second you're aware of how little time you have left.

The waterfront entry to the BART is locked. A hand-lettered sign proclaims the underground tunnel linking San Francisco and Oakland is too dangerous to pass. Max looks to his left, then right. People on the street are rushing by chaotically. No one pays any attention to the two of you. Max takes four steps back and makes a running charge at the locked gate. With a loud clang the thin metal chain snaps in half. Together you and Max enter the dark tunnel. Ollie whines and sits down at the entrance, refusing to go any farther.

"You keep watch for us, boy," says Max. "We'll be back soon."

Turn to page 101.

Ellsworth sends you into the next room to search for some towels. Ollie stays close by your side. By the time you return, Zooey's delivered two very furry little tigers which she licks roughly, but in a motherly way. Sitruc stands next to her, looking proud and calm.

Four days later the mayor presents you and Max with keys to the city. Your help in delivering the baby tigers has made national news. You and Max—and Ollie—are considered the earthquake's heroes. But the real hero is Dr. Orion, who wins the Whitbread Prize for his innovative report on animal behavior immediately preceding major earthquakes. He generously presents both you and Max with ten-speed bikes as thanks for your help after the earthquake.

"It's the least I can do," he says. "You saved my life, and Zooey's too. I'll never forget you."

You leave for home happily, knowing you'll never forget Dr. Orion, or your adventures in San Francisco, either.

The End

"Ten minutes is ten minutes," you announce after a moment's thought. "My gut reaction says we should take the shortcut."

"Your gut reaction is good enough for me," Max says.

"Great," C.W. answers. "Follow me." With that she revs her accelerator and zooms onto the deserted highway. You throw the motorcycle into gear and follow. "These police bikes can really move," you shout to Max.

About a mile and a half farther up Highway 101 C.W. pulls off onto a rugged dirt road and you do the same. The first jolt of dirt nearly throws you to the ground. Ollie begins barking frantically. Thankfully, you recover in time and decrease your speed. You'll have to watch for stones that could send you headfirst over the handlebars, you think. Judging from Max's python grip around your waist, you're certain he's having similar thoughts.

The road winds up and down, around sharp corners and through heavy vegetation. You struggle to keep C.W.'s motorcycle in view. She really knows how to handle these back roads.

Turn to page 111.

Your only shot at getting back into the Lion House, you decide, is tricking the gorilla into moving the boulders aside. Slowly you walk backward toward the boulders, all the while keeping a guarded eye on the ape. The gorilla watches you with obvious interest. He pauses for a moment, trying to gauge your actions. Then he continues to walk toward you. You hope he can't sense your fear.

You reach the large boulders and begin to move behind them. There is a narrow crawl space between the two largest rocks. You squeeze in there. The remaining boulder is at your back. Listening intently, you hear the footsteps of the gorilla as he approaches your hiding spot.

Turn to page 72.

"I'm going to get help," you say hurriedly to Dr. Orion. "I'll leave Ollie with you and Max."

With that you're off, racing toward the research building in the hope of locating someone—anyone—to help. But when you get there, the building is as empty as you left it before.

You run through the building where you met Brewster earlier. Suddenly you fall flat on your face—you've tripped over a snake! You are very relieved to see it's only the garter snake Brewster was feeding. There's no sign of Brewster, though. He must have left the zoo before the earthquake hit.

Retracing your steps, you circle back toward the Bear Grotto. As you turn the corner, your knees give out. For a moment you think you've tripped over another snake, until you realize it's the earth that is moving. A strong aftershock rocks the ground around you. You listen in terror as you hear what sounds like a building collapsing. The Lion House, you think in horror. You jump to your feet and begin running as fast as you can to help your friends Max and Dr. Orion.

Turn to page 99.

"We'll draw less attention to ourselves by taking the boat," you say. "Besides, who knows what condition the roads are in?"

"I suppose you're right," Max agrees.

"Follow me," you say quietly. Together you stroll down to the pier and approach the boat. It's a small Boston Whaler with an eighty-horsepower engine. Not the fastest boat in the world, but it'll have to do.

You climb on board as if you own it. Max follows, keeping a discreet eye on the police officers above. You have some trouble getting Ollie to come on board, but finally he hops in. You look over the starting mechanism of the speedboat and disengage a few engine wires. You touch the ends of the positive and negative connections together and the engine races to life. You step aside and let Max expertly maneuver the boat out onto the open water. Max's dad recently bought a thirty-foot schooner, and Max has become quite adept on the water. So far, so good, you say to yourself.

Turn to page 76.

Just as you reach the door of the building, a screeching siren perched high atop a pole begins to wail. The sound is deafening. No doubt it can be heard for miles surrounding the town. You've made it in time to warn everyone. Within seconds people begin to pour out of buildings, looking confused and disoriented. With a growing sense of urgency they head toward the town square. C.W. and the police chief step outside and watch with you.

"That shortcut really saved us time," you say to her appreciatively. C.W. turns to smile. The siren is so loud that you wonder if she heard what you said.

Just then the concrete steps of the city hall begin to shake, faster and faster, throwing you off balance. A loud rumble replaces the sound of the siren. It sounds like a beast from the center of the earth, howling in anger. You struggle to stay on your feet. Ollie huddles against you. You know this is just the beginning.

The End

You're no match for the gorilla, and you know it. You'll have to find another way into the Lion House. A loud roar comes from inside the building. It sounds like Sitruc. Dr. Orion and Max must really be in trouble.

The gorilla watches you cautiously for a few more moments. Deciding you aren't a threat after all, he lumbers away. You make certain he's gone and then circle the building, looking for a way in.

About halfway around the exterior you spot a small window that looks like a ventilation opening near the roof. It's your only hope. You drag a bench over to the wall and turn it on end. It rests a few feet below the window. You climb up the bench and precariously balance on the end. Bending your knees gently, you prepare to make a lunge toward the window. The bench shifts slightly, forcing you to throw your arms out for balance. It stops moving, and you act quickly. You leap up, throwing the weight of your body into the jump. With arms straight above your head, you grab at the window. You make it! Your hand grasps a metal handle just as the bench crashes to the ground below you.

Turn to page 102.

The next morning Ollie seems all right, so you decide to keep your appointment with Professor Bailey. Even if Ollie's behavior has something to do with seismic activity, you think it would be best to see Professor Bailey. Her methods of earthquake prediction seem more reliable than the ones Max has told you Dr. Orion uses. If an earthquake *is* coming, you figure that Professor Bailey will be the first to know.

"Let's take Ollie to the lab with us," you say to Max. "We'll keep an eye on him there. We can still take him to the zoo later in the afternoon."

"Okay," Max agrees reluctantly.

At nine o'clock sharp you, Max, and Ollie step off the elevator at basement level D of the WhitVic Research Center. You ring the buzzer, and Professor Bailey opens the door. "Right on time," she says in greeting. "I like people who are punctual."

"Hi," you say. "This is my friend Max." Ollie jumps out from behind Max and licks Professor Bailey's hand, wagging his tail wildly. The professor laughs, surprised.

"Nice to meet you, Professor Bailey," says Max. "My dog Ollie has been acting a little strange lately and we didn't want to leave him alone. I hope it's okay for him to be here."

Professor Bailey shakes Max's hand and then Ollie's paw. "It's quite all right, Max," she says. "But we do have some delicate equipment. Maybe Ollie could wait for you in the hall."

Turn to page 81.

You and Max silently stare at each other for a moment. You turn back to the captain. "We have to pass under the bridge," you shout. "We have to get to San Rafael as soon as possible."

"I wouldn't if I were you," the captain yells back. "Even if the bridge doesn't get you, the waves from its fall will flip your boat over like a burger on a grill."

"What do you say?" Max asks you quietly. "I don't think we have a choice."

You squint at the bridge. It seems so peaceful, swaying back and forth in the wind. If you're going to go under it, you'd better do it now. Otherwise, you'll have to start looking for an alternate route.

*If you choose to go under the bridge,
turn to page 12.*

*If you decide to try an alternate route,
turn to page 89.*

You approach Zooey cautiously. She's obviously in great pain. You fall to your knees and listen to her rapid heartbeat. After calculating her heart rate you call out to Dr. Orion, "It's over a hundred and twenty beats per minute."

"And her breathing," he calls back, concerned.

You listen closely. Her breathing sounds labored, as if she were gasping for air. "Not good," you reply.

"You have to move her," Dr. Orion says with urgency. "The tiger cubs are in distress. Put your hands under her hind legs and slowly rotate her onto her side."

You glance at your watch. Only three minutes have gone by since Ollie left. It feels like an eternity. Following Dr. Orion's orders, you slip your arms beneath Zooey's hind legs and gently turn her over.

Turn to page 71.

Professor Bailey continues the tour of the lab, explaining the function of various machines and their data-tracking methodology. "All the research is stored on a mainframe computer up on the second floor in the data collection center," she says. "Would you like to go up and see it? I'll telephone Professor Potter to tell him you're friends of mine. He'll show you around."

Thanking Professor Bailey, you collect Ollie, who is whining once again, and take the elevator up to the lobby. You're heading for the stairs when you stumble. You look down to see what tripped you and you realize that the floor is moving.

"Oh, no—not another tremor!" you call out to Max.

Turn to page 82.

As much as you hate the thought of touching the snake, you realize that Max is right. The second you made a grab at the lemurs, the adder would strike—most likely at you. You're just going to have to stick with the original plan. Narrowing your eyes in concentration, you approach the snake very slowly.

The adder momentarily turns away from the lemurs and eyes you. It opens its mouth and bares its fangs. You do everything in your power to keep from turning around and running. The snake closes its mouth and begins moving in a circular pattern again. This time it seems to be deciding the exact moment to lunge at you.

Turn to page 69.

As you're drifting off to sleep you hear Ollie walking around and around the room. "Lo mein," you sigh, and pull the pillow over your ears.

You wake with a sudden start. The room is completely dark, but you're sure you heard a strange noise. You hear it again. It's whining, and it's coming from the corner. "Ollie, boy," you whisper. "Are you okay?"

You turn on the bedside lamp and watch Ollie with concern. He's pacing back and forth at the other end of the room. He doesn't even look up at you but continues to whine to himself.

"Max," you say in a loud whisper. Your friend stirs in his bed and sits up, rubbing his eyes groggily. "I think something's wrong with Ollie."

Turn to page 14.

"No," Professor Bailey says in a harsh whisper. "Leave me for the rescue squad. They'll find me. I need you both to do something much more important." She's quiet for a moment as she gathers the strength to speak.

"The second floor—the data collection center," she gasps. "Go there and read the emissographs. This wasn't the Big One. This was just a foreshock. The emissograph with the highest radon reading will tell you where the Big One will hit, probably later today. You have to go warn people."

"Professor Bailey," you plead, "we can't just leave you. What if they don't find you? What if you just lie here—"

"Never mind me," she commands. The strength in her voice surprises you. "We're talking about saving hundreds of people, not just me. Now hurry."

You look at Max who looks back at you, shaking his head. You've got to do something, and fast.

If you follow Professor Bailey's plea and go to the data collection center, turn to page 74.

If you carry Professor Bailey to safety, turn to page 23.

You think Dr. Orion is pretty weird, but he seems nice enough. You, Max, and Ollie say good-bye and begin the walk to Professor Bailey's lab.

Soon after leaving the zoo you pass a corner grocery store. "Let's stop in here and get Ollie a bone," Max says. "He seems upset again. Maybe a snack would calm him down."

Just as you step out of the shop, Ollie suddenly stops in his tracks and stares up at you, fear in his eyes. He lets out a loud bark.

"What is it, boy?" Max asks, concerned. Just then a deathly silence settles over the city as a slow rumble from deep within the earth begins to build and build.

The pavement beneath your feet starts to sway. You throw your arms out for balance. You feel like you're surfing—and about to crash into the biggest wave of your life. Terrified, you look toward Max.

"Hang on," he yells over the thunderous rumble. "It's an earthquake—a big one!"

Turn to page 87.

Suddenly one of the lemurs leaps away from the adder. The snake turns away from you for a split second, distracted by the sudden movement. This is your chance! You leap forward and grab the adder by the neck. It thrashes about in your hand, struggling to break free. Its tail snaps back and forth wildly.

"Grab the tail," Max yells. "Do it now!"

You swiftly grasp the adder's tail and pull it straight. The snake's skin is dry and smooth, not slimy as you'd expected, and you're able to hold on.

"Over here," says Max. Looking over, you see that he's emptied a large plastic bucket of the lemurs' food. He suspends the cover two inches above the empty pail and holds it out to you through the crack in the cage. You race toward him, throw the snake into the bucket, and watch as Max slams the lid down. You've done it! The lemurs are safe. But will you be in time to help Dr. Orion?

The End

"She's gone into shock," Max yells as you place Professor Bailey's stretcher down carefully. Quickly turning around, Max runs toward the mouth of the alley. You keep pace.

"Over here, over here," you scream as you spot a member of a rescue squad. Two emergency medical team members descend on Professor Bailey. They listen for her pulse, then hook her up to an IV. One begins to administer CPR while the other blows air into her lungs. After several frantic minutes, Professor Bailey sputters and coughs, then begins to breathe normally once again. Ollie licks her hand happily.

"You boys saved this woman's life," one of the team members tells you. "You have a lot to be proud of."

You motion toward the alley entrance. "Now on to the data collection center," you whisper to Max. Ollie jumps up and runs to your side. You only hope you have enough time to read the graphs and warn people before the Big One hits.

The End

You've just rolled Zooey onto her side when an aftershock rumbles through the Lion House. You hear more walls crumbling, but the crashing sounds distant and Zooey's area sustains no further damage. You stroke the tigress's ears. Her breathing sounds a little better now.

After a few more excruciating minutes of waiting there is a commotion at the room's entrance. Glancing up you see Ollie enter, followed by a tall, thin man dressed in blue overalls. It worked! Ollie is gripping the man's overalls in his mouth, dragging him forward. "All right, all right," the man says.

Dr. Orion calls out weakly from the darkened corner, "Ellsworth Parris! I've never been so glad to see you in all my life." Ellsworth turns toward Dr. Orion, his face registering deep concern.

"Don't worry about me," Dr. Orion tells him. "It's Zooey over there I'm concerned about."

Somewhat reassured, Ellsworth hurriedly enters the tiger cage. He doesn't seem the least bit frightened of Zooey or Sitruc.

"It's a good thing that darn dog of yours is so tenacious," he says to you. "I was trying to capture a loose bat and he just wouldn't let go of my leg. I knew there had to be real trouble somewhere in the zoo—and he led me here."

The whole time he's been talking Ellsworth has been gently patting Zooey's stomach and taking her pulse. You breathe a quick sigh of relief. Zooey is in good hands now.

Turn to page 48.

72

Suddenly he sees you between the rocks and lets out a high-pitched yell. He's angry now. He swipes his hand through the space between the rocks. He can almost reach you, but not quite. You make a grunting noise, hoping it sounds like anger. With any luck he'll buy the challenge and shove the rocks aside to get at you.

It works. The gorilla begins to claw at the rock immediately in front of you. Just as you guessed, his overwhelming strength allows him to move the boulder at will. The gorilla shoves the rock aside quickly. Suddenly you are exposed. You scramble backward, trying to find a crawl space behind the third rock. You throw yourself to the ground and slither behind it. It's a tight fit, but you make it.

Turn to page 80.

You bundle up several lab coats and place them beneath Professor Bailey's head. "There," you say gently. "That should make you more comfortable." Ollie nudges her hand, and she strokes his nose weakly.

"We promise," Max says quietly, "that as soon as we get outside we'll send someone right down."

"I'll be fine," Professor Bailey says. "Just hurry!"

The tone in her voice means business. You follow Max out the door and toward the stairwell. Ollie follows at your heels. You begin climbing upward, picking your way through the rubble and destruction of the quake. All this destruction— and it's from just a foreshock? You can only hope Professor Bailey's wrong about her prediction.

Turn to page 95.

You rev the motorcycle and head north toward the Golden Gate Bridge. When you reach it, you find the bridge in surprisingly good shape. It's also clear of traffic. You zoom ahead. The wind rushes past your ears. It almost sounds like a siren.

"They're following us," Max yells. "Step on it." In your rearview mirror you watch as another police motorcycle begins to gain on you.

Turn to page 106.

Max steers out into the bay and begins heading north toward the Bay Bridge. The police don't seem to notice your departure. The waters are fairly choppy as a result of a stiff northerly wind. Max pushes the engine toward its upper limit. You climb forward to get a better look at the gas gauge.

"Only a little above a quarter tank," you say, pointing to the control panel. "I hope we don't run out." Max pushes up the accelerator and steers carefully.

The pounding waves beat against the bow of the boat. It feels as if you're hitting concrete. The constant banging is giving you a headache. Ollie's anxious barking isn't helping, either.

"Uh-oh," Max says as he slows the boat down. "Looks like trouble up ahead." In front of you, several large tugs pull at metal cables attached to the Bay Bridge. The middle portion of the bridge sways in the wind. The tension from the cables appears to be all that is keeping it from collapsing. Max pulls alongside one of the barges. You wave at the barge captain to attract his attention.

"The bridge looks in bad shape," you yell. He stares at you for a moment and nods in agreement.

"Couldn't be worse," he yells back. "The quake snapped all the major grounding cables. The middle section could fall in any second. And when it does, you'd better watch out, 'cause the rest will follow like a line of dominoes."

Turn to page 59.

You reach the waterfront only to find the road blocked off by several police officers standing next to their motorcycles. Frustrated, you try to talk your way past the barricade, but the police won't hear of it. You try to tell them about Professor Bailey's research and the impending danger to San Rafael, but they don't believe you. After listening to you for a few moments, one of the officers humors you by asking where he can get in touch with Professor Bailey to verify your story. You begin to explain that she's unconscious and that you don't know her exact location at the moment. The officers laugh heartily. You can tell they think you're just a couple of kids telling a tall tale.

Frustrated, you, Max, and Ollie start to walk away. Suddenly you spot a motorboat anchored to a fishing pier down below.

"Psssst," you whisper to Max. "Down there. The small boat. I could hot-wire the engine."

"It'll take too much time," Max whispers back. "Our only option is over there." He motions with his head. You follow his eyes.

"The cop's motorcycle?" you ask. "Are you kidding? We'd get arrested and land in jail."

Go on to the next page.

"Who cares about jail?" Max asks impatiently. "We have to go warn some people about a major earthquake—before it strikes!"

You've got to decide which plan will get you to San Rafael the fastest: the boat, or the motorcycle?

If you choose to hot-wire the boat, turn to page 54.

If you choose to grab the policeman's motorcycle, turn to page 94.

The gorilla screams in anger at your quick escape. He grasps the third boulder with his large hands and begins to rock it back and forth, trying to shove it aside.

Frantically, you feel behind you with your hand, trying to locate the door handle for the room that holds the cage. Nothing is there! There's no door handle, no door. Did you miscalculate? You could have sworn the door was right behind you.

The gorilla screams with all his might. He senses victory. A few more shoves of the rock, and you'll be his.

You keep a watchful eye on the gorilla while trying not to panic. Making an effort to kneel, you feel the wall behind you. There has to be a door here someplace, you think to yourself. You can hear your heart beating rapidly against your ribs. You feel as if you can't breathe.

The gorilla grunts loudly one last time and shoves the rock aside. He eyes you in anger, takes a step back, and beats his chest furiously. He bares his teeth and hisses. He's got you cornered. You'll never escape. It was a good idea, but it didn't work. The gorilla raises his enormous hand above you. As it swoops toward you, you shut your eyes in terror—for the last time.

The End

The seismology lab is cool and dark. Professor Bailey shows you the seismographs, which measure the earth's undulatory motions, and the emissographs, which measure radon gas from points all over California. She also introduces you to her colleague Chamberlin Wurtenberg, a tall, thin woman with flaming red hair and millions of freckles.

"Chamberlin Wurten . . . Wurten . . ." you say, stumbling over her name.

"My friends call me C.W. for short," she says, gripping your hand tightly. "You should, too." She smiles brightly, putting you at ease.

Professor Bailey points to a graph measuring radon in the San Rafael area. For several inches there are straight lines, and then a series of jagged ones. "This came in late last night," Professor Bailey says with obvious excitement.

"What does it mean?" Max asks.

Turn to page 88.

"Earthquake!" Max screams. He dives for you and pushes you into the doorway of one of the labs. With Ollie cowering between you, you brace yourselves in the doorframe, waiting in terror for the deafening rumbling to end. All around you windows shatter like balloons burst with pins. The floor seems to be moving up and down, up and down—like turbulent waves at the ocean. Then, as suddenly as it began, the earthquake is over. The rumbling noise stops, and Ollie ceases barking. All is ominously quiet.

"I guess the quake came earlier than Professor Bailey expected," Max says.

"We've got to make sure she's all right!" you say. "Come on—this way."

Max and Ollie follow you down the broken concrete stairs to the basement. The hallways are deserted. A backup generator powers a small, dim light overhead.

Turn to page 38.

You swallow hard and turn toward the lemurs. The puff adder is dangerously close to them. It is moving its head in a small circular pattern, as if choosing the exact moment it plans to strike. You take several deep breaths and cautiously begin to approach the snake. "Now remember," Max whispers from outside the cage, "gently, but quickly, grasp the adder's head and squeeze."

You look over at the lemurs. They seem so close. If you could just grab them and slip back through the glass opening, you'd never even have to deal with the snake. You do have extremely fast reflexes. And you really hate snakes.

Guessing what's on your mind, Max says quickly, "Don't even think about it. You'd never make it. You have to grab the snake."

If you decide to grab the lemurs and exit, turn to page 35.

If you decide to grab the adder, turn to page 63.

Five miles farther there's a makeshift roadblock with a sign reading "DANGER—ROAD CLOSED AHEAD."

"Now what?" you yell to Max. Ollie pants in the sidecar, looking as if he wonders why you stopped.

After a moment's pause, he answers. "There was a side road back just a little ways. I've taken it before: it's pretty rough but it brings you right up next to the Richmond–San Rafael Bridge. If we take it, we should be able to bypass the closure."

You suppose he's right. "But what if the bridge is damaged?" you ask.

"No way," he replies confidently. "That bridge was designed to be earthquakeproof. The side road will take us right there."

"But we'll waste time doubling back," you say. "Why don't we run the roadblock?"

"We're wasting time standing here," Max says. "Let's make a decision and go!"

If you run the roadblock, turn to page 96.

If you go back and take Max's side road, turn to page 108.

An earthquake! You're so stunned you can't move. This is just what you've been fearing! Max grabs you and hangs on for dear life. Ollie leans against you, trembling in fear. You hear a whistling sound, and then a crash. You turn around and see that the large metal grocery store sign has fallen off the roof of the building and narrowly missed crushing you!

Turn to page 24.

"We're not sure," C.W. replies. "But if our theories about prediction are right, it could mean—"

Just then one of the seismograph's needles starts to jump up and down furiously. All four of you run toward the machine. The needle jumps for a few more seconds, then calms down.

"That one was about a three point three on the Richter scale," says Professor Bailey. "It was somewhere off the coast—probably about sixty miles out."

"An earthquake?" you ask, swallowing hard.

"A very minor one," C.W. replies. "They happen all the time. You get used to them out here." Where have I heard *that* before? you think.

Turn to page 62.

"I doubt we'd make it," you say. "Besides, we're low on gas. Even if we did get to the other side, if the bridge fell we'd never have enough fuel to ride out the waves. We need to think of some other way to get to San Rafael."

"I have an idea," Max says, circling back. You can tell by the gleam in his eye it's going to be a good one. "We'll drop this boat off near Fisherman's Wharf," he says. "Then it's on to BART."

The wind is screaming past your ears. You can barely hear. "Did you say Bart?" you yell. "Who's he?"

"Not who," Max replies. "What. The BART is Bay Area Rapid Transit. The subway. Trust me."

Turn to page 47.

As you move to downshift into second gear, you slide across a patch of rough gravel. Ollie barks wildly and jumps out of the sidecar. You try to adjust your balance and increase the accelerator.

It's too late. The bike is in a full slide toward the steep embankment, and you and Max are being dragged along.

The bike continues to lurch ahead. You can't stop it! You try to dig your feet into the ground, but it's no use. The bike lurches over the side of the embankment, with you still gripping the handlebars and Max gripping you around the waist. Ollie barks at you from the edge.

For a moment everything is quiet. You have a dreamy sense of flying. Above you is a cloudless, dark blue sky. After a second you realize the San Rafael Bridge has broken in two. Both sides dangle precariously from the sides of the crevasse. Then you look down. Two hundred feet below you is a dry riverbed. It gets closer and closer and closer. You shut your eyes in terror as you, Max, and the bike fly through space to the riverbank below.

The End

Max's words frighten you. With a sudden increase in energy, you begin to push even harder. The speed of the cab increases.

But the water seems to be getting deeper. It becomes harder and harder to push the cab ahead. You begin to slow in despair. "Keep moving," Max barks. "We're at the low end of the tunnel. If we can go another five hundred feet we should be able to climb out of this mess."

The water gets deeper and deeper until you can no longer move ahead. The sound of rushing water increases. You're directly underneath one of the bulbs. Looking around, you can see the water climbing up the wall. "We're heading directly toward the flow!" you wail.

Max looks up and down the tunnel. There's no way out. "We'll have to swim for it," he shouts. "We should head back. At least we know the leak wasn't behind us." Max jumps off the cab and begins to swim toward the exit. Fighting a growing sense of panic, you follow.

It's no use. The depth of the water continues to grow. There is only about a foot between the top of the tunnel and the water. Frantically you swim ahead. The flow of the water increases. Within minutes your head is touching the ceiling. "Don't stop," Max yells back. "It can't be much farther."

Turn to page 113.

But the fire fighter didn't know about C.W.'s shortcut. You find out later that C.W. got through in time to warn the people of San Rafael about the earthquake. She shares the credit for saving the town with you and Max, and the three of you are hailed as heroes. Professor Bailey doesn't go unrecognized, either. From her hospital bed she accepts the Whitbread Prize for her lifesaving research. You return home, happy that you don't live near any major fault lines.

The End

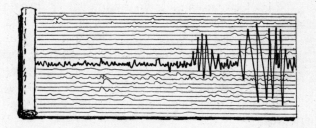

"You're right," you whisper to Max. "Let's take the cycle." You look around nervously. A woman approaches the police officers and begins to gesture wildly. When she begins yelling something about trying to find her cat, you make your move. Casually and quietly you amble over to the motorcycle, hop aboard, and grasp the key. Max is about to climb into the sidecar when Ollie leaps in ahead of him and sits there, thumping his tail.

"Attaboy, Ollie! Looks like you're along for the ride." Max jumps on behind you and you race the engine, flying off at lightning speed. In your rearview mirror you watch the police look up in complete surprise.

"We did it!" Max yells in your ear. "Hey, where'd you learn how to drive one of these things?"

"Drew Kellet," you yell back. "A guy down the street in Vermont." What you fail to add is that you only rode on Drew's motorcycle twice—and only as a passenger. But you're a quick learner, and you manage to get on your way with little difficulty.

Turn to page 75.

You reach the second floor, where Professor Bailey's data collection center is located. The exit door is jammed shut by a fallen piece of concrete. With you pushing and Max pulling, you're able to move the concrete off to the side. You run through the door, Max and Ollie two steps behind you.

The seismology laboratory is a wreck. Overturned tables and chairs, smashed computer equipment, and broken glass are everywhere. Miraculously, two of the emissographs are still humming away. They must have backup emergency generators up here, too, you think. You run to the first one. There's bunch of small lines with a sudden jolt about the time of the quake, then nothing. Then you begin reading the tape on the second machine.

Turn to page 44.

Max grips your waist even tighter as you accelerate through the roadblock to make up for lost time. Ollie cowers in terror in the sidecar. This ride must be more than he bargained for.

Your speed climbs to sixty-five miles per hour. Inside you have a terrible sinking feeling. What if you're too late? You push the thought aside and slow down to take a sharp corner in the road.

Just around the bend you spot a large fire truck parked sideways across the road. There's no way around it. You slam on the brakes and nearly fly over the handlebars as you screech to a halt. A startled fire fighter approaches.

Turn to page 105.

Two miles past the Mill Valley exit C.W. pulls off to the side of the road. Confused, you stop behind her, keeping your engine on idle.

"What's up?" you shout above the engine's roar.

"If I'm not mistaken, there's a shortcut up ahead on the left. It should save us about ten minutes," she replies. "We used to take it when I was a kid."

"What do you mean, if you're not mistaken?" Max asks in doubt. He strokes a shaking Ollie.

"Well, let's just say I'm almost one hundred percent certain that's the way to go," she replies.

You haven't got much time to waste. A shortcut might get you there faster. On the other hand, if you get lost, you'll never make it in time to warn the people of San Rafael. Maybe you should stay on the main highway.

It looks as if C.W. and Max are divided about what to do. It's up to you to decide.

*If you decide to take the shortcut,
turn to page 50.*

*If you decide to stay on the main highway,
turn to page 103.*

A cloud of dust is just settling around the Lion House as you sprint toward it. Part of the structure has collapsed, but another part is still intact. Frantically you race to the building, hoping that Dr. Orion and Max are okay. You locate the area where you think the door should be. Several large boulders block the area. You struggle to push them aside. But it's of no use. You're not strong enough to move them by yourself.

In desperation you look around. A large male gorilla, sitting on his haunches about fifteen feet away, stares at you. He looks as if he weighs about six hundred pounds. The gorilla suddenly stands up, beats his chest, and grunts. He acts as if you're trespassing in his territory and he's got to do something about it. Suddenly you get an idea. It's risky but it just might work. If you could crawl behind the boulders and hide, the gorilla might try to find you. With his strength, he could probably shove the boulders aside, giving you a way back into the Lion House.

You eye the gorilla nervously. He lets out a frightening hiss and takes three steps toward you. He's awfully big. Maybe you should find another way in.

If you try to lure the gorilla behind the boulders, turn to page 51.

If you decide to find another way into the Lion House, turn to page 57.

Leaving Ollie behind, you and Max sneak down one of the tunnel paths toward the main tracks. You're in luck! Near the end of the east-bound track sits an old, hand-powered repair cab. Only a few remain in the city, most having been replaced by computer-controlled digital speed cabs. You jump on board and begin seesawing the power lever back and forth. The cab creaks into motion. This is certainly not the fastest means of transportation, but you have no choice.

The tunnel under the bay is almost pitch-black. Every so often there is a small emergency bulb illuminated by a backup generator. You can't see between bulbs; all you can do is head for the next one.

About a quarter mile into the tunnel you begin to hear running water. You seem to be heading toward it.

Another five hundred yards farther up the tracks you not only hear the water, you feel it as well. Cold water begins to lap at your ankles. You slow your pace for a second. "Do you think it's flooded up ahead?" you ask Max fearfully.

"Doubt it," he replies, out of breath. "My guess is there's a minor leak somewhere. Still, we'd better hurry before the pressure of the leak breaks into a full-blown river."

Turn to page 92.

102

You swing your feet onto the ledge. In front of you is a small window, probably used for cross ventilation. Grabbing the handle with both hands, you struggle to open the window. But it won't budge. Gripping the window frame, you kick at the glass with your foot. It shatters, leaving a dangerously jagged opening.

Inside the building you hear Sitruc growl again. Cautiously you lower yourself through the shattered glass. You drop to your feet on the cold stone floor, get your bearings, and move toward Zooey's cage. For a moment you struggle with the door, which has been jammed shut in the aftershock. Finally, after several hard slams with your shoulder, it bursts open.

Turn to page 109.

"Almost certain isn't good enough," you say thoughtfully. "What if you're wrong? Or what if that back road's all ripped up? I say we stay on the main highway."

"Okay," C.W. agrees. "I see your point. But just to be sure, I'll take the shortcut, you two take the main road. With any luck, one of us will get there in time." She doesn't even wait for you to reply. She pulls off the shoulder and throws her bike into second gear, zooming toward the shortcut. You pull out after her and watch as her cycle disappears to the left.

About two miles farther up the main highway you begin to encounter some rough road. Cautiously you maneuver through several small roadslides, no doubt caused by the previous quake. You're forced to slow your speed to around twenty miles per hour, causing you to lose precious time.

"Can't you go any faster?" Max asks impatiently.

"Not if we want to get there in one piece," you answer. "You wouldn't want Ollie to fall out." You downshift into first gear and weave around a large boulder. Finally, the road seems to clear a little, and you're able to pick up some speed.

Turn to page 85.

"Yahoo!" Max yells, and Ollie barks joyously. You open your eyes. You've made it! You're now about fifteen feet past the bridge, and you're still alive.

"There's a little island with a gas station up ahead," Max says triumphantly. "We have enough to make it there to refuel. Then it's on to San Rafael."

"Aye, aye Captain," you yell back, grinning from ear to ear. You can't stop the earthquake from happening, but if your luck holds out you'll be in time to sound the alarm and save some lives.

The End

"Didn't you see the sign back there?" she asks angrily. "You could have rammed into the truck!"

"We're in a hurry," you answer impatiently. "We have to get to San Rafael to warn them . . ."

"Well you can't get through on this highway," she cuts in quickly. You get off the bike and Ollie dances around your legs in delight because the ride's over.

"Come on," says the fire fighter. You follow her around the back of the fire truck. Max gasps in horror. Ahead of you is a seventy-foot-wide crevasse where the bridge to San Rafael once stood.

"It came down in the quake," says the fire fighter. "There's no way into San Rafael."

Turn to page 93.

You push the motorcycle as fast as it'll go, but without any luck. The motorcycle behind you is only twenty yards back. With incredible speed it pulls up on your right. Looking over, you spot the insignia of the San Francisco Police Department. You've been caught! You look up at the officer driving.

"C.W.!" Max yells. "Quick, pull over."

Sure enough, C.W. is the driver. Once you've pulled to a stop, she glides in next to you. Ollie barks in greeting.

Turn to page 112.

108

You hope Max is right about the bridge. You turn the cycle around and head back to the side road. About a quarter mile up the road Max taps you on the shoulder and points to your left. You exit off the main highway onto a narrow dirt road.

You keep your speed at a steady pace. You have to swerve several times to miss small boulders or avoid large potholes. Max wasn't kidding when he said the road was rough. You begin to sweat from nervousness. You realize that off-road and highway riding are two very different things. Ollie whines and leans his head out, looking at the road.

"It should be just up ahead," Max yells in your ear. "About another two hundred yards or so."

You don't seem to be near any river or embankment. The trees are still thick around you. You wonder what this bridge crosses.

Suddenly, as if a curtain has been pulled back with a yank, you emerge from the woods into a wheat field. You can tell there is a steep embankment to your right. The wheat is very tall. It's harvest time, you realize. You can barely see where you're going.

"Slow down a little," Max cautions. "I need to get my bearings."

Turn to page 90.

As you step into the Lion House, Ollie lets out a yelp of joy at seeing you. You glance over at Dr. Orion and Max. Max shakes his head sadly.

Approaching the animals you realize that Zooey is lying very still. Sitruc gently licks her face, but there is no heavy breathing, no movement. Gently you pull Ollie aside and let Sitruc mourn Zooey by himself. It's too late for you to do anything else.

Just then a slow rumble begins to build from deep within the earth's core. You lean dejectedly against the wall and wait for the aftershock to pass.

The End

After only a few miles, the rugged road begins to smooth out. Within minutes you're approaching a town. The few farmhouses along the way are now replaced with smaller homes placed closer together. The town looks completely untouched by the earthquake. The smoothness of the road allows you to accelerate. Within seconds you've pulled alongside C.W.

"Which way?" you shout.

"Straight ahead," she yells back. "There should be an earthquake alarm at the police station." She picks up speed. You follow.

Ahead on your right you spot an official-looking brick building—the city hall and police station. C.W. pulls off the street and into the parking lot. She doesn't even wait for you to get off your bike. She charges ahead into the building to sound the alarm. You dismount and break into a run after her. Ollie and Max are at your side.

Turn to page 55.

"How did you know where we'd gone?" you ask C.W. as she removes her motorcycle helmet.

"I caught sight of you running toward the waterfront," she replies. "I saw Professor Bailey when they brought her out of the building. She told me about sending you to the data collection center."

"How's the professor?" you ask quickly.

"Okay," C.W. replies. "Couple of bad breaks though."

"But how did you find us?" asks Max.

"When I saw you hop the motorcycle," she explains, "I just grabbed the other. Boy, were the police surprised!"

"I'll bet," you reply. At least you'll know your cell mates when they throw you in jail, you think to yourself.

"Well—where will the Big One hit?" she asks.

"San Rafael," you reply. "The lines nearly jumped off the graph."

With that, you're off, C.W. in front, you just seconds behind. Max grips your waist in terror. You're flying down the highway at an incredible speed. You're surprised Ollie doesn't fly out of the sidecar. At this rate you should reach San Rafael in a matter of minutes.

Turn to page 98.

Just then a loud swishing noise comes from behind you. The water streams over the top of your
head, carrying you forward. You can't see. Help-
lessly you're pushed ahead with the current. You
can only assume that Max is in front of you.

You struggle for several seconds, but it's
useless. You give yourself over to the flowing
water. A strange sense of serenity engulfs you. A
vision of your family passes before you. You shut
your eyes to savor the image. It's the last thing
you'll ever see.

The End

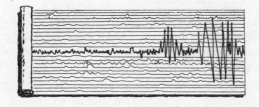

ABOUT THE AUTHOR

ALISON GILLIGAN graduated from New York University, where she majored in art history. She worked in the art auction business and with an advertising agency in New York City before moving to Seattle, Washington, where she currently resides. Ms. Gilligan recently edited a Northwest art catalog and is currently working on a screenplay. Her previous book in the Choose Your Own Adventure series was *The Treasure of the Onyx Dragon*.

ABOUT THE ILLUSTRATOR

HAL FRENCK studied at Syracuse University. He has worked at several advertising companies, most recently BBDO in New York. While Mr. Frenck has illustrated books for many different publishers, *Earthquake!* is his first Bantam Choose Your Own Adventure book. He lives in Fairfield, Connecticut.

CHOOSE YOUR OWN ADVENTURE®

JOIN THE

The exciting series from the creator of
CHOOSE YOUR OWN ADVENTURE®

Join the universe's most elite group of galactic fighters as you make your moves in this interactive series—
SPACE HAWKS!
Meet your fellow space travellers and become a part of the faster-than-light action.

Each **SPACE HAWKS** adventure is illustrated by comic book artist Dave Cockrum!

ORDER SPACE HAWKS TODAY!

____	28838-5	FASTER THAN LIGHT (#1)	$2.99/$3.50C
____	28839-3	ALIEN INVADERS (#2)	$2.99/$3.50C
____	28899-7	SPACE FORTRESS (#3)	$2.99/$3.50C
____	28961-6	THE COMET MASTERS (#4)	$2.99/$3.50C
____	29355-9	THE FIBER PEOPLE (#5)	$2.99/$3.50C
____	29406-7	THE PLANET EATER (#6)	$2.99/$3.50C

Bantam Books, Dept. DA-42, 414 East Golf Road, Des Plaines, IL 60016

Please send me the titles checked above. I am enclosing $ _____
(please add $2.50 to cover postage and handling).
Send check or money order, no cash or C.O.D.s please.

Mr./Ms _____

Address_____

City/State _____ Zip: _____

Please allow 4-6 weeks for delivery   DA-42 3/92
Prices and availability subject to change without notice.